MY BARK IS THE BEST PART!

A RHYMING STORY FOR TINY ANIMAL LOVERS

Author Zoe Walker
Illustrator Elizaveta Borisova

I'd like to dedicate the book to 5 amazing children who inspired this book - Lara, Aiden, Zoe, Isabelle and Hannah

Hello, I am your new puppy, Zali Rose.
I have tiny ears and a triangle nose.
I love to run, play, cuddle and eat.
You will see, I'm so cute and sweet.

You'll love my soft fur and tiny tail too.
But there's one thing I need to tell you.
I am still a baby as you used to be.
So, please, be kind and patient with me.

I am a little bit scared, in a new place.
My family is away with no trace.
I miss my mom and siblings too.
All the family I have now is – you!

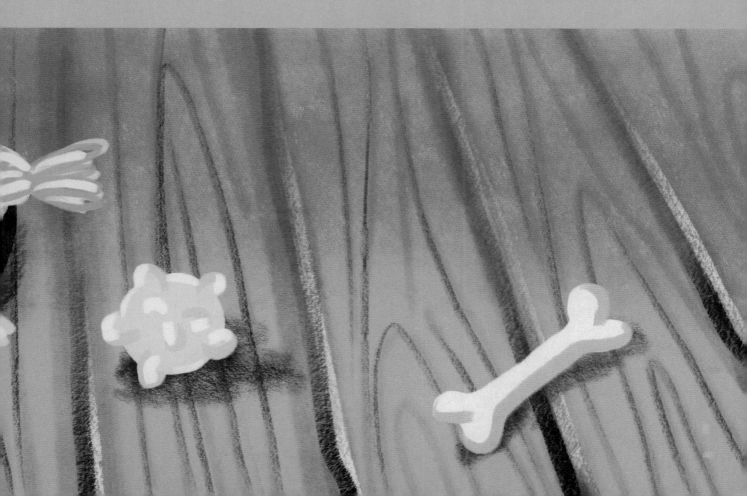

At first, I could be naughty or yappy.
Please, understand I'm just a puppy.
You will hear my baby paws at night,
because I miss mom's hug to sleep tight.

I'll tell you the cure for my fear.
Please give me a scratch behind my ear.
Throw me a ball, take me to the park.
I can't say thank you, but I sure can bark!

I like plush toys, and teddy bears too.
Don't be mad if I take them from you.
I love to pull their ears, by the way.
Sorry if I break them during the play.

My tiny teeth grow, and I need to chew.
Forgive me if I eat your sock or
maybe a shoe.
I might accidentally have an oopsy
in your room.
It most likely won't smell like perfume.

I'll try to steal your lunch if it's yummy.
Always remember - I have a hungry tummy.
I can't eat your tasty cakes and sweets,
but I adore dog biscuits and treats!

I don't do these things to hurt you.
It's just something that puppies do!
With a lot of your love and
unconditional care,
I'll grow into a good dog.
I promise - I swear!

I have many more things I need to learn,
but I will give you so much in return.
It won't always be easy, but in the end,
I will become your best friend!

Made in the USA
Monee, IL
04 November 2021